S0-ABA-655

Harry Gets an Uncle

by Barbara Ann Porte
pictures by Yossi Abolafia

HarperTrophy®
An Imprint of HarperCollinsPublishers

Watercolor paints and a black pen were used for the full-color art.

HarperCollins®, 🍎®, HarperTrophy®, and I Can Read Book® are
trademarks of HarperCollins Publishers Inc.

Harry Gets an Uncle
Text copyright © 1991 by Barbara Ann Porte-Thomas
Illustrations copyright © 1991 by Yossi Abolafia
Printed in the U.S.A. All rights reserved.
www.harperchildrens.com

Library of Congress Cataloging-in-Publication Data
Porte, Barbara Ann.
    Harry gets an uncle / by Barbara Ann Porte ; pictures by Yossi Abolafia.
        p.   cm. — (An I can read book)
    Summary: Harry is worried about being the ring boy at his aunt Rose's wedding, after he
hears his friend Dorcas tell horror stories about what went wrong at her uncle Fred's
wedding.
    ISBN 0-06-001150-5 — ISBN 0-06-001151-3 (lib. bdg.) — ISBN 0-06-001152-1 (pbk.)
    [1. Weddings—Fiction.]   I. Abolafia, Yossi, ill.   II. Title.
PZ7.P7995Han   1991   90-39562
[E]—dc20   CIP
                                                                             AC

First Harper Trophy Edition, 2002
Originally published by Greenwillow Books,
an imprint of HarperCollins Publishers, in 1991.
❖

I, Harry, am going to a wedding.

"I'm getting married, Harry,"

my Aunt Rose said.

"Mr. Baxter will be your Uncle Leo."

"Congratulations," I said.

"I've never had an uncle before."

Aunt Rose and I have known
Mr. Baxter for a long time.
He plays the tuba in Red Rose Quintet,
Aunt Rose's five-piece band.
Aunt Rose sings and plays the piano.

I tell my friend Dorcas the news.

"I've never been to a wedding," I say.

"Really?" she says.

"I went to a wedding once.

My Uncle Fred got married.

It was awful."

"Awful how?" I ask her.

Dorcas tells me.

"There were a zillion relatives,"

she says. "Most of them

I'd never seen before.

They pinched my cheeks and said,

'Isn't she sweet? My how she's grown!'

I was the flower girl.

My dress was long and hot and prickly.

It tripped me whenever I walked.

The flowers were roses,

with thorns that stuck me.

Losing the ring was the worst part."

"You lost the ring?" I ask.

"It was my brother Billy's fault,"
Dorcas says.

"Carrying the ring was his job,
but he came down with chicken pox.
'You're next in line,'
my Uncle Fred told me.
'But I'm the flower girl,' I said.
'Dorcas will be glad to do both,'
my mother told him.

"I walked down the aisle carefully,
holding the roses in one hand
and the wedding band,
on a velvet pillow, in the other.

"Just as I got to the altar,

the pillow tilted.

The ring slipped off it,

rolled under a table,

and stuck in a crack in the floor.

"The entire wedding party

wound up on their hands and knees

underneath the table,

looking for the ring.

After they found it,

they couldn't get it out.

"Uncle Fred borrowed my mother's ring
and married Aunt Esther with it.
After the ceremony,
they moved the table
and pried up the ring with a fork.
It's still a little bent.
Believe me, Aunt Esther wasn't pleased.

"The next week,

while she and Uncle Fred

were on their honeymoon,

I was home in bed

with chicken pox."

"I think I'll skip Aunt Rose's wedding,"

I tell my father that night,

"and stay at home with Girl."

(Girl is my dog.

She lives with my Aunt Rose

because my father is allergic,

but she's spending

their honeymoon with us.)

"Skip?" my father says.

"You're Aunt Rose's ring boy."

"No one told me that," I tell him.

"I just did, right now," he says.

"Anyway, if you stay home,

you'll be at the wedding.

Aunt Rose is getting married here,

in our backyard."

"How will everybody fit?" I ask.

"Everybody who?" my father says.

I tell him what Dorcas told me.

"When her Uncle Fred got married,

a zillion people came."

"So far as I know," my father says,

"the only people coming here

are a few close relatives and friends."

"Yes, but what about the ring?" I ask.

I tell him what happened to Dorcas.

My father sighs.

"Please, Harry," he says.

"Believe me, such a thing

won't happen twice."

Right, I think, but something else

could happen, even worse.

"Your aunt could move away
and take Girl with her,"
Dorcas says when I tell her.
"That would be worse."
"Why would she want to do that?"
I ask.
"Most people move away
after they get married,"
Dorcas explains.

"My Uncle Fred, for instance,

lived next door to us

until he got married.

Then Aunt Esther saw an ad

in the paper.

'Circus Help Wanted,' it read.

'I've always wanted to be

in the circus,' she said.

It turned out, so had Uncle Fred.

They both got jobs selling tickets.

Now Aunt Esther's a clown.

Uncle Fred feeds the elephants

and hoses them down.

The only time we see them

is when the circus comes to town."

After school, I visit my Aunt Rose.

"Hi, Harry," she says.

"I'm glad you're here.

I can use a hand with the dusting."

We start on her piano.

Girl puts her front paws

on the bench and watches.

"What's on your mind, Harry?"

Aunt Rose asks.

"You look a little worried."

"Who, me?" I answer.

Girl yawns.

"I think Girl's worried

about where she'll live

when you move away,"

I tell Aunt Rose.

Aunt Rose looks surprised.

"I'm not moving anyplace," she says.

I tell her what Dorcas told me.

"I see," says Aunt Rose.

"*Some* people move after they get marrie

Uncle Leo, for instance.

When we get back

from our honeymoon in Bermuda,

he's moving in here."

I'm glad to hear it.

That's when I bring up the ring.

"I've decided to carry it in my pocket,"

I tell Aunt Rose.

"I think that way,

I probably won't drop it."

Aunt Rose smiles.

"Don't worry," she says.

"I'm sure you won't.

I only hope it doesn't rain.

That would be awful."

Yes, I think.

The guests would get wet.

The cake would
be ruined.

Fortunately, Aunt Rose's wedding day
is sunny. Benches have been put
in the yard. The cake and food

have been set out on long tables.

Beside the dogwood tree,

there is a canopy.

They will be married underneath it.

Girl is safely inside the house
when the guests begin arriving.
"My, how Harry has grown,"
a few of them say.
So far, no one has pinched my cheek.

The musicians from Aunt Rose's band

are here: Luke, on bass;

the drummer, Lucille;

and Herbert, who plays French horn.

The music begins.

I put my hand in my pocket

to be sure the ring is still there.

I hold on to it tightly.

Uncle Leo's niece, Denise,

walks down the aisle first,

holding the flowers. I go next.

After me come the bridesmaids
and ushers, and then Uncle Leo
and my father, who is best man.

The band swings into

"Here Comes the Bride."

Aunt Rose starts down the aisle,

holding on to Grandpa's arm.

She is dressed all in white,

with a train and a veil.

Aunt Rose looks beautiful.

The guests all smile.

Then some of them begin to giggle.

I see why.

Girl is walking down the aisle,

right behind Aunt Rose and Grandpa.

I wonder how she got out of the house.

When Aunt Rose and Grandpa

stop beside Uncle Leo,

Girl keeps going.

She sits in the shade

of the dogwood tree

and watches the ceremony.

Part way through it, just as I am about

to hand Uncle Leo the ring,

Ms. Parker's cat, Tulip,

who lives next door,

squeezes through the fence

to see what's going on.

Girl sees her, barks, and runs over.

Tulip sees Girl.

She puts up her back and hisses.

Then she dashes for the dogwood tree,

with Girl at her heels.

Tulip races up the tree trunk.

She stretches out on a

high branch and looks down.

Girl sits at the foot

of the tree and looks up.

The wedding has come to a standstill.

No one seems to know what to do.

Uncle Leo clears his throat.

"Harry," he says. "If you have the

ring, I think the wedding can

proceed."

I hand him the ring.

He winks at me.

He doesn't look even a little angry.

He puts the ring on Aunt Rose's finger

and kisses her. The band begins to play.

I take Girl inside the house.

Ms. Parker comes over from next door
and coaxes Tulip down from the tree.
"I'm so sorry about the disturbance,"
she says to Aunt Rose.
"It was a lovely wedding, anyway,
and you are a beautiful bride."

Then, holding on to Tulip
with one hand,
she reaches out with the other
and pinches Aunt Rose's cheek.

All the guests are eating and talking and dancing.

Aunt Rose and I, Uncle Leo
and my father, Denise and her parents
join hands and dance together
in a circle.

When the wedding is over
and the guests have gone home,
Uncle Leo gives me a wristwatch.
"It's to thank you," he says, "for being
such a good ring boy and nephew."
"Thank you," I tell him.

"How was the wedding?"

Dorcas asks the next day

when I show her my wristwatch.

"Fine," I say.

"I didn't drop the ring.

Ms. Parker's cat caused a disturbance,

but other than that,

nothing bad happened.

We all had a very good time.

Even Girl did."

A few days later, a postcard

arrives from Bermuda.

On one side is a picture

of Aunt Rose and Uncle Leo, waving.

On the other side, it says,

"We're having a wonderful time.

We miss you all.

Give Girl a pat for us.

Love, Aunt Rose and Uncle Leo."